Make Way for Dumb Bunnies

Story by Sue Denim · Pictures by Dav Pilkey

SCHOLASTIC INC.

New York Toronto London Auckland Sydney

To my loving husband,
Rev. Darryl F. Denim S. D.

For Kevin Lewis D. P.

ISBN 0-590-58288-7

Text copyright © 1996 by Sue Denim
Illustrations copyright © 199603 by Dav Pilkey
All rights reserved. Published by Scholastic Inc.

12 11 10 9 8 7   08 09

Printed in the United States of America   08
First Scholastic paperback printing, October 1998

The illustrations in this book were done with watercolors, India ink,
acrylics, gouache, skim milk, and Vick's Vap-O-Rub.

This book was originally published in hardcover by the
Blue Sky Press in 1996.
Original Blue Sky Press edition designed by Dav Pilkey
and Kathleen Westray

Early one morning, the Dumb Bunnies were spending some quality time apart.

Poppa Bunny was watching the Super Bowl,

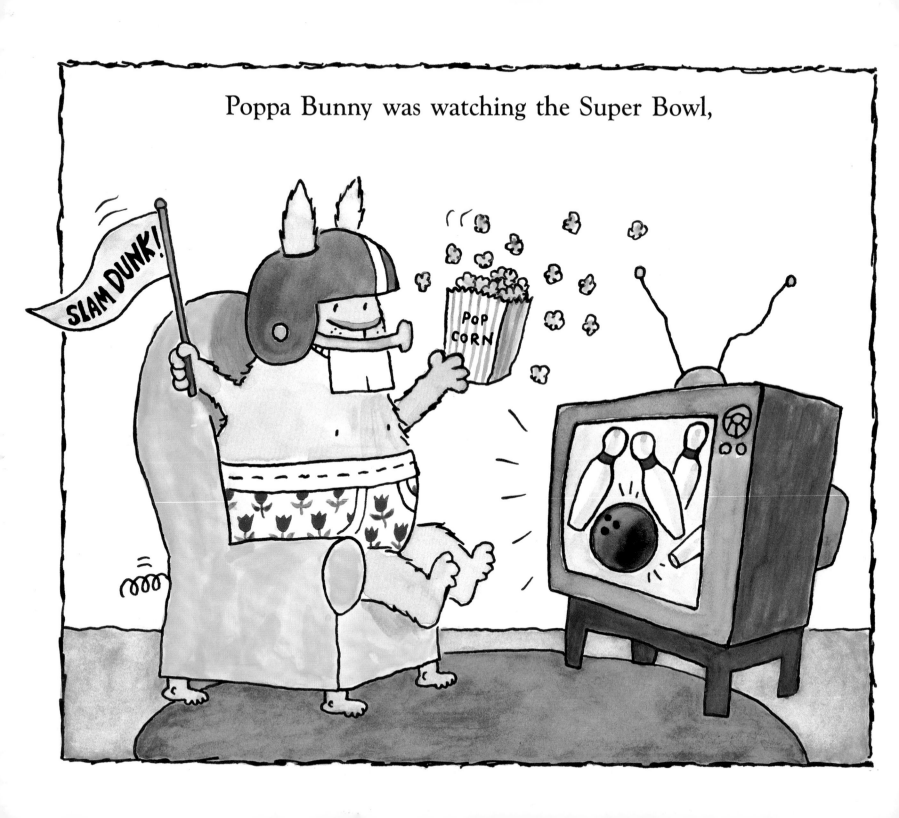

Momma Bunny was watching the Orange Bowl...

...and Baby Bunny was watching the Toilet Bowl.
"That's my boy!" said Poppa Bunny.

Soon it started to rain. Dark clouds rolled in, and thunder flashed brightly all around.

"It looks like a *perfect* day to go to the beach," said Poppa Bunny.

So they packed three sack lunches...

...loaded up the car with everything they needed,

and headed off for the beach.

When they got to the beach, the Dumb Bunnies
went in for a swim.

Baby Bunny took his umbrella, because
he didn't want to get wet.

Afterwards, Momma Bunny combed the beach,

Poppa Bunny went fishing in a boat…

...and Baby Bunny blew up an inflatable raft.

"That's my boy!" said Poppa Bunny.

Soon the rain stopped, and the sun came out.
"Looks like bad weather," said Momma Bunny.
So the Dumb Bunnies headed back to town.

On their way, they came across the deal of the century!
"Duh, look!" said Poppa Bunny. "A free car!
Let's take it!"

So they did.

When the Dumb Bunnies got to town, they parked
their new car and went to see a movie.

Inside the lobby, they bought a tub of popcorn.

But the Dumb Bunnies didn't enjoy the movie very much.

"The screen is too small," said Poppa Bunny.
"And it's too *bright*," said Momma Bunny.

After the movie, the Dumb Bunnies could hardly see a thing.

They looked all over for their new car.
"Duh, I think I found it," said Poppa Bunny.
So they all climbed in and drove toward home.

It was a very bumpy ride.

At last, the Dumb Bunnies arrived home safe and sound.

It was getting late and was almost time for bed.
"Can I watch TV in my pajamas?" asked Baby Bunny.

"Dokey-Okey," said Momma and Poppa Bunny.

So Baby Bunny put the TV in his pajamas
and watched it all night long.

"That's my boy," said Poppa Bunny.